Original Korean text by Bo-geum Cha
Illustrations by Hanneke Nabers
Korean edition © Yeowon Media Co., Ltd.

This English edition published by big & SMALL in 2016
by arrangement with Yeowon Media Co., Ltd.
English text edited by Joy Cowley
English edition © big & SMALL 2016

Distributed in the United States and Canada by
Lerner Publishing Group, Inc.
241 First Avenue North
Minneapolis, MN 55401 U.S.A.
www.lernerbooks.com

All photo images used are in the public domain, except:
page 37 "Scenes from contemporary performances of The Nutcracker" -
left © Xomenka (CC BY-SA 3.0),
right © Alexander Kenney & Kungliga Operan (CC-BY-3.0)

ISBN: 978-1-925247-38-1

Printed in Korea

Tchaikovsky's

The
Nutcracker

Retold by Bo-geum Cha Illustrated by Hanneke Nabers
Edited by Joy Cowley

big & SMALL

On Christmas Eve, snow falls over Clara's house
where people are gathering for a festive party.
It's a night when something magical might happen,
a night of color and music and strange surprises.
Let's go to Clara's house and join the party…

Mr. Drosselmeyer

He is a family friend.

Clara

She is the daughter
of the house.

Prince

He is the
Nutcracker.

Fritz

He is Clara's
younger brother.

Mouse King

He is one of the
strange surprises.

Sugar Plum Fairy
and
other fairies

They are from the Land of Sweets.

6

On Christmas Eve, the tree shone with decorations.
The children played in the living room
while the adults chatted and laughed.
Clara and her brother Fritz were having fun inside
while outside the window snow fell heavily
as the day deepened into night.
Suddenly, someone threw open the door.

"It's Mr. Drosselmeyer!" shouted Clara.
"I've waited all day for him to come!"

Mr. Drosselmeyer had wrinkles and a patch on one eye,
and whenever he came he brought toys for the children.
He put a box on the floor. "You can open it!" he said.
Out of the box came soldiers, a clown, a singing doll,
and toys that danced or turned cartwheels.
The children clapped their hands in excitement.

The last thing in the box was a Nutcracker doll.
It was an ugly wooden soldier with a big head.
Clara gently touched it and said, "I want it!"

But Fritz snatched the Nutcracker doll from her.
He was so rough, he broke it.

Clara's eyes brimmed with tears. "That was my doll!"

"I will fix it for you," said Mr. Drosselmeyer.
Carefully, he put the Nutcracker together again.

The party ended and the guests went home,
but Clara found it difficult to get to sleep.
She crept downstairs to see the Nutcracker.
"My poor Nutcracker! I'll look after you."
She held the Nutcracker in her arms,
and he stared at her with big, sad eyes.

Ding, ding, ding, ding...
The clock chimed midnight.

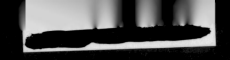

On the stroke of midnight, something strange happened.
The toy soldiers got bigger and came alive.
The Nutcracker also grew big and tall.
As they moved across the living room,
a swarm of mice appeared from holes in the walls.
"This is our place," they said. "Get rid of the soldiers!"
Fiercely, the army of mice attacked the toy soldiers.

The brave Nutcracker led the toy soldiers,
urging them, "Forward! We will not be defeated!"
Bang, bang! Boom, boom! Squeak, squeak!
The noises of guns, cannons, and mice all mixed together,
but the mice kept coming. There was no end to them!
The Mouse King was big with seven ugly heads,
and he ran at the Nutcracker, waving his sword.
"We'll get this one first!" he yelled.

All this time, Clara had been hiding behind the sofa.
Now she stood up, quickly took off a slipper
and threw it with all her might at the Mouse King.
The slipper hit him, and he staggered back.
This was the Nutcracker's chance to leap forward.

When the Mouse King was injured
by the Nutcracker's sword,
he called to the mice, "Let's get out of here!"
Away they scuttled, vanishing into the dark.

Clara looked around.

The toy soldiers were dancing, enjoying their victory,
and Clara, to her great surprise, was now in a beautiful dress.
As for the Nutcracker, he had turned into a prince.
The prince put the Mouse King's crown on Clara.
"Thank you for helping us, Clara," he said.
"If it wasn't for you, we would have been in big trouble.
Would you like to come to my country,
the beautiful Land of Sweets?"

Some secret stairs appeared behind the cupboard door.
Hand in hand, Clara and the prince walked down them,
and eventually they came out to a bright new world
where sweet-smelling sugar fell like white snow.
They crossed a honey-filled river in a nutshell boat
and arrived at a castle made of sweets, almonds, and chocolate.
"Everything is so beautiful!" cried Clara.

The Sugar Plum Fairy, surrounded by many other fairies, welcomed Clara to the castle and invited her inside.

"I owe my life to Clara," said the prince. "She helped me when we were almost beaten by the Mouse King."

The fairies took Clara to the best seat at the table and brought out plates of cookies and sweets.

A welcome party for Clara began.
The Chocolate Fairies danced to the beat of castanets,
and the Coffee Fairies swayed to soft music.

When the prince poured Clara some hot tea,
the Tea Fairies appeared, waving their fans.

The Reed-Pipe Fairies danced to flute music,
their feet hardly touching the ground.
The Candy Cane Fairies did an energetic dance,
kicking up their long, striped legs.
Clara watched them with shining eyes.

"This party has been truly wonderful,"
Clara said to the prince.

"It's not over yet," he said.
"Look at the Flower Fairies."

The Flower Fairies drifted in with harp music.
They performed a beautiful, colorful dance,
moving like petals in a gentle breeze.

After the Flower Fairies,
the Sugar Plum Fairy entered with a young knight.
They danced elegantly together.
The Sugar Plum Fairy spun lightly around,
and the knight lifted her high in the air.
It was brilliant dancing!
But then the music died away,
and it was time to leave the party.
Clara said goodbye to the prince.
"We won't ever see each other again."

"That's not true," he said. "I'm your friend.
I know that one day we will meet again."

Clara woke up to a bright Christmas morning.
She hugged the Nutcracker that lay beside her.
"My prince!" she said.

At that moment, her mother walked in.
"Did you sleep well, Clara?" she asked.
"You look like you had a happy dream."

Clara just smiled at her mother.
Was it only a dream? Clara didn't think so.

♪: Let's Learn About **The Nutcracker**

🎵 Pyotr Ilyich Tchaikovsky

Born: 7 May 1840
Died: 6 November 1893
Place of birth: Votkinsk, Russia
Biography: Tchaikovsky was a famous Russian composer whose works included symphonies, concertos, operas, and ballets. His musical talent was obvious from his first piano lessons at the age of five. However, it was not until he was twenty-two that he enrolled in the Saint Petersburg Conservatory to study music. After graduating from the conservatory, he started his career as a professional composer. Tchaikovsky composed works in which Russian melodies were mixed with European music techniques. Tchaikovsky's ballet music is especially praised for being well-organized and artistic. Tchaikovsky's three major ballet works, *Swan Lake*, *The Sleeping Beauty*, and *The Nutcracker*, are still performed all over the world. Tchaikovsky died in 1893, shortly after finishing his *Symphony No. 6 in B Minor*, which was played at his funeral.

Mariinsky Theater where *The Nutcracker* premiered

The Story of **The Nutcracker**

The Nutcracker was based on the story *The Nutcracker and the Mouse King* written by a German writer called Ernst Theodor Amadeus Hoffmann (1776–1822). Hoffmann practiced law during the day, but spent his nights writing. A choreographer named Marius Petipa adapted Hoffman's story and asked Tchaikovsky to provide the musical score for the ballet *The Nutcracker*.

The premiere of *The Nutcracker* was held at the Mariinsky Theater in Saint Petersburg on the 19 March 1892. The first performance wasn't successful as it received a lot of negative criticism for not being faithful to Hoffmann's fantastic tale. It later became very popular after the story and choreography were changed. For a concert performance, Tchaikovsky selected some of the music from the ballet and formed *The Nutcracker Suite, Op 71a.*

A drawing of a costume for *The Nutcracker*

Scenes from contemporary performances of *The Nutcracker*

♫ Let's Find Out About the Music

When Tchaikovsky started composing *The Nutcracker*, he suffered from writer's block.
Nothing inspired him to write the composition. To make matters worse, he then heard that his beloved sister Sasha had died. However, on his way to attend Sasha's funeral, his inspiration returned.
In the Sugar Plum Fairy, he created a parallel for his sister. Memories of their childhood helped him to compose the music, and he imagined himself as the character Mr. Drosselmeyer.
The Nutcracker is loved by children and remains the most popular ballet performed during the Christmas season. Let's find out about the music and the magical atmosphere of this ballet.

Miniature Overture

This piece of music announces the beginning of the ballet. It is mainly played by musical instruments with light tones. The violins lead the melody.

March

The trumpets, horns and clarinets dominate the opening. Their commanding sounds announce the beginning of the march. Listening to the melody of the first and second violins, you can imagine children playing in a house filled with Christmas decorations.

Arabian Dance

The sound of cor anglais (a woodwind instrument similar to an oboe) and clarinets express the exotic mood. Its slow, memorable melody is accompanied by the elegant movements of the dancers. This music is famous for reflecting the flavor of coffee.

Chinese Dance

In the Land of Sweets, Clara is given a cup of tea. The bassoons and double basses represent the boiling water. The flute solo mimics the sound of pouring the tea into the cup.

♫ Let's Find Out About the Music

Dance of the Reed-Pipes

A trio of flutes carries the melody, accompanied by pizzicato strings — plucked with a finger, rather than played with a bow. This represents reeds in the wind. The light, "bouncing" sound of the flute is most memorable part of this music.

Trépak

From the beginning to the end, the tempo (speed) increases to a very fast level, and then ends abruptly. In the ballet performance, the Candy Cane Fairies are dancing to this energetic, speedy music. It's based on a traditional Ukrainian folk dance in which male dancers squat down and repeatedly kick out. The exciting, trembling sound of the tambourines is the characteristic feature of this piece of music.

Waltz of the Flowers

In the ballet performance, dancers move gracefully to the music. Opening with a harp solo, the music becomes richer and richer, as melodies of horns and woodwinds are added to the strings. While listening to this flowing piece, you can imagine the well-dressed dancers' beautiful waltz at a wonderful ball.

Dance of the Sugar Plum Fairy

After arriving in the Land of Sweets, Clara and the prince are greeted by the Sugar Plum Fairy. For this piece, Tchaikovsky used a musical instrument which was new at the time called a celesta (a type of keyboard, similar to a piano). The instrument gives a special magic to the "Dance of the Sugar Plum Fairy".